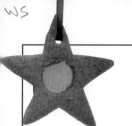

What shall I cook?

Ray Gibson

Designed by Amanda Barlow

Edited by Fiona Watt

Illustrated by Sue Stitt

Photographs by Howard Allman

Series Editor: Jenny Tyler

Food stylist: Ricky Turner

With thanks to Julia Kirby-Jones

Contents

Before you start any of the recipes in this book, make sure that you have all the things you will need. Always ask someone to help you to switch on your oven to the correct temperature, before you begin to cook. Also ask for help when you put things into an oven or take things out of it. Wear a pair of oven gloves before you pick up anything which might be hot.

Chocolate octopuses

For 10 octopuses, you will need:
125g (4oz) soft margarine
125g (4oz) caster sugar
1 medium egg
3 tablespoons of cocoa powder
175g (6oz) plain flour
sweets for eyes
greased baking tray

For butter icing:
25g (1oz) butter
50g (2oz) icing sugar
lemon juice

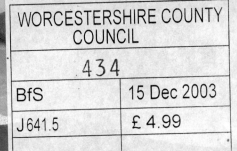

WORCESTERSHIRE COUNTY COUNCIL	
434	
BfS	15 Dec 2003
J 641.5	£ 4.99

1. Mix the sugar and margarine in a bowl with a wooden spoon until they are creamy.

2. Sift the flour and the cocoa into the bowl. Add the egg and mix them well to make dough.

3. Use your hands to press the dough into a large ball. Wrap it in plastic foodwrap.

4. Put the wrapped dough into a freezer for 30 minutes or into a fridge for an hour.

    Heat the oven to gas mark 5, 190°C, 375 °F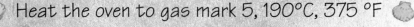

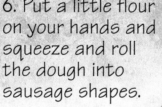

5. Cut the dough in half. Put half of it back into the fridge. Divide the rest into five pieces.

6. Put a little flour on your hands and squeeze and roll the dough into sausage shapes.

7. Gently flatten each shape then use a blunt knife to make four cuts for legs.

8. Gently pull the legs apart. Pinch their ends into points and bend them out.

9. Take the other half of the dough out of the fridge and make five more octopuses.

10. Lift the octopuses onto a baking tray. Bake them for 10-12 minutes.

11. Leave them to cool for a little while before putting them on a cooling rack.

12. Follow step 8 on page 21 to make icing. Put some icing on the sweets. Press them on for eyes.

Jam tarts

For about 12 tarts, you will need:
150g (6oz) plain flour
75g (3oz) margarine
6 teaspoons of very cold water
pinch of salt
jam
greased baking tray with shallow pans
round cutter
tiny cutters

Making pastry

1. Mix the flour and the salt. Rub in the margarine so that it looks like crumbs.

2. Add the water. Use a blunt knife to mix it in. Squeeze it into a ball of dough.

To make the tarts

3. Sprinkle flour onto your work surface. Roll out the dough thinly.

4. Press out 12 shapes from the dough with the round cutter.

If you haven't got any tiny cutters use a bottle top instead.

Heat the oven to gas mark 6, 200°C, 400°F

5. Push the shapes into a greased tin. Put a teaspoon of jam into each one.

6. Press out some shapes with the tiny cutters. Put one on each tart.

7. Bake the tarts for about 15 minutes in your oven.

8. Take care as the tarts will be very hot. Leave them to cool on a rack.

Wait until the tarts are cold to eat them.

What shall I cook today? Cheesy snakes and caterpillars

For about eight snakes and four caterpillars, you will need:
150g (6oz) self-raising flour
½ teaspoon salt
25g (1oz) margarine
75g (3oz) cheese, finely grated
1 egg and 2 tablespoons of milk, beaten together
raisins for eyes
a bottle top
greased baking tray

1. Sift the flour and salt. Add the margarine and rub it with your fingers to make crumbs.

2. Leave a tablespoon of cheese on a saucer. Add the rest to the bowl and stir it in.

3. Put a tablespoon of the egg mixture in a cup. Mix the rest into the flour to make dough.

4. Roll out the dough on a floury surface, until it is as thick as your little finger.

5. Use a blunt knife to cut eight strips as wide as two of your fingers.

6. Bend the strips into wiggles. Pinch the ends. Press one end flat for a head.

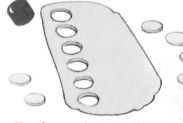

7. To make a caterpillar, cut out six circles of dough with a bottle top.

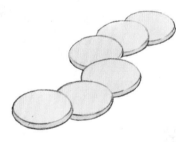

8. Lay the circles in a line. Overlap the edges and press them together.

9. Brush the shapes with the egg mixture. Sprinkle with cheese. Add raisins for eyes.

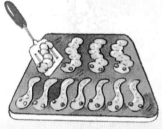

10. Use a fish slice to lift the shapes onto a greased baking tray.

11. Bake for about eight to ten minutes, until they are golden.

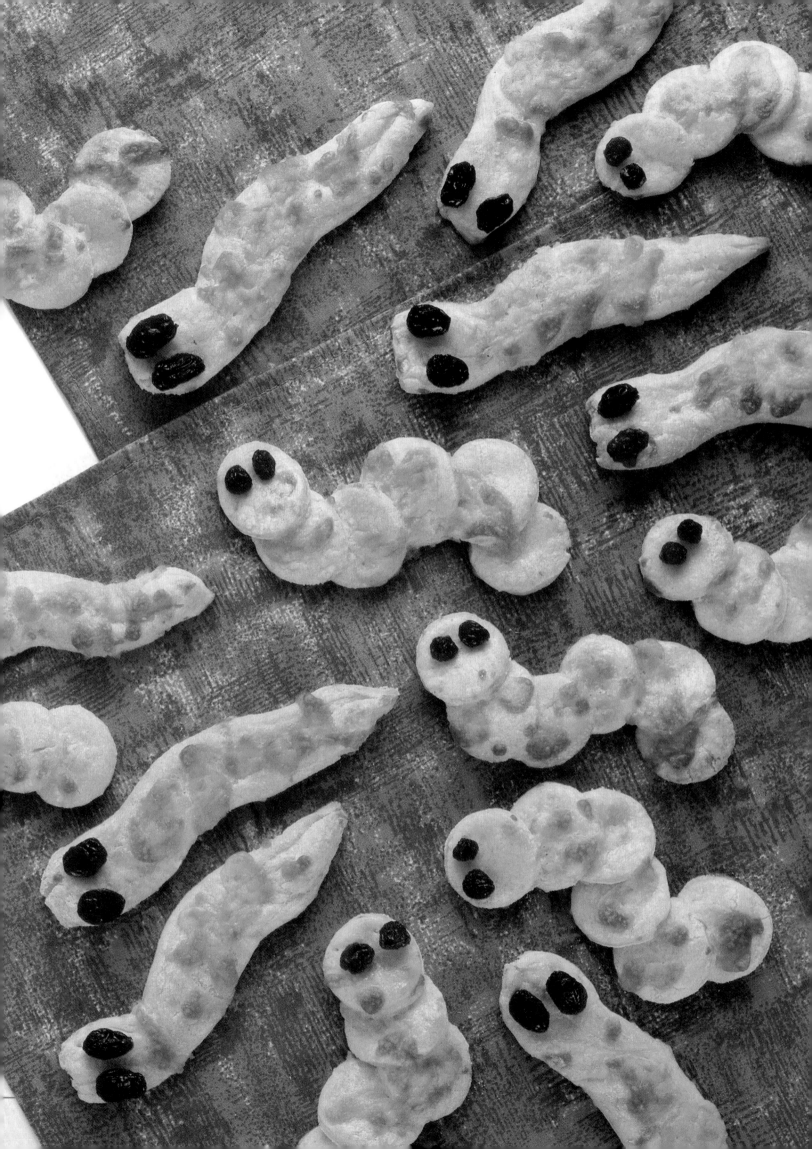

Owl cakes

For ten owls you will need:
225g (8oz) wholemeal flour
½ teaspoon of ground cinnamon
2 level teaspoons of baking powder
75g (3oz) margarine
50g (2oz) demerara sugar
1 medium-sized cooking apple, chopped finely
1 egg, beaten
10 glacé cherries, chopped in half
whole blanched almonds
raisins
greased baking tray

1. Sift the flour, cinnamon and baking powder together in a bowl.

2. Cut the margarine into lumps. Add it to the bowl. Rub it in with your fingers.

3. When the mixture looks like crumbs mix in the sugar, apple and egg.

These owls are delicious if you eat them warm with ice cream.

Heat the oven to gas mark 6, 200°C, 400°F

4. Lift out a heaped tablespoon of the mixture. Put it on a greased baking tray.

5. Squeeze the mixture to make a body shape. Make nine more owls.

6. For eyes, press in two pieces of cherry. Add an almond for a beak.

7. Bake the owls for about 15 minutes, until they are golden brown.

8. Let the owls cool for a few minutes then put them on a rack.

9. When the owls are cool, press a raisin into the middle of each eye.

Upside-down pudding

This pudding is made upside-down with the topping at the bottom of the dish. You turn it over once it has cooked.
For the sponge, you will need
100g (4oz) self-raising flour
2 eggs
100g (4oz) caster sugar
100g (4oz) soft margarine

For the topping, you will need:
25g (1oz) butter
400g (14oz) tin of apricot halves, drained
glacé cherries
50g (2oz) brown sugar
20cm (8in) ovenproof dish

For the sponge:

1. Sift the flour into a big bowl. Add the eggs, margarine and caster sugar to the bowl.

2. Stir everything together with a wooden spoon until you get a smooth creamy mixture.

For the topping:

3. Grease the sides of a baking dish. Melt the butter. Pour it all over the bottom.

4. Use your fingers to sprinkle the brown sugar evenly on top of the butter.

5. Put the apricots around the edge, cut-side up. Fill in the middle. Put cherries in the gaps.

6. Spread the sponge over the fruit. Bake on the middle shelf for 45 minutes.

Ice cream goes well with this pudding.

7. Loosen the edges with a knife. Turn the pudding upside-down onto a big plate.

Eat the pudding while it is still warm.

You could use thick slices of cooking apples, tinned peaches or pineapple rings.

Shining star biscuits

For about 24 biscuits you will need:
60g (2½oz) soft brown sugar
60g (2½oz) soft margarine
half a small beaten egg
125g (5oz) plain flour
1 teaspoon ground mixed spice
solid boiled sweets
large cutter
small round cutter, slightly bigger than the sweets
a baking tray lined with baking parchment
fat drinking straw

You can use any shape of boiled sweet.

1. Mix the sugar and margarine really well, getting rid of any lumps.

2. Mix in half of the beaten egg, a little at a time. You don't need the other half.

3. Sift in the flour and the spice. Mix it really well with a blunt knife.

4. Squeeze the mixture together with your hands to make a firm dough.

5. Roll out the dough on a floury surface until it is 5mm (¼in) thick.

6. Press out star shapes. Use a fish slice to put them on the baking tray.

7. Make a hole in each star by pressing the straw in one of the points.

8. Use a small cutter to cut out a shape in the middle of each star.

   Heat the oven to gas mark 4, 180°C, 350°F

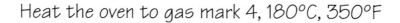

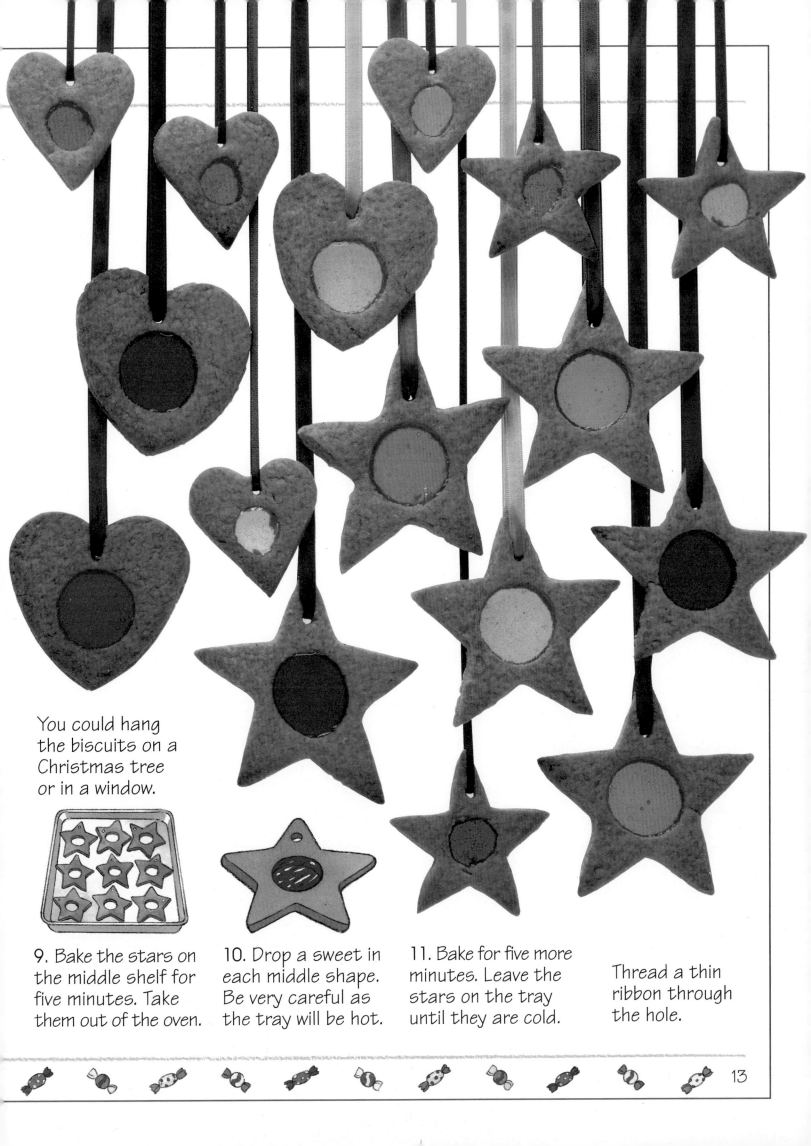

You could hang the biscuits on a Christmas tree or in a window.

9. Bake the stars on the middle shelf for five minutes. Take them out of the oven.

10. Drop a sweet in each middle shape. Be very careful as the tray will be hot.

11. Bake for five more minutes. Leave the stars on the tray until they are cold.

Thread a thin ribbon through the hole.

Apricot muffins

For 12 muffins, you will need:
100g (4oz) self-raising flour
50g (2oz) wholemeal flour
1 level teaspoon of baking powder
1 level teaspoon of ground mixed spice
75g (3oz) dried apricots, chopped
110ml (4floz) milk
50g (2oz) butter, melted
1 large egg
2 teaspoons of lemon juice
75g (3oz) soft brown sugar
muffin tin, well oiled

1. Sift the self-raising flour. Add the wholemeal flour and baking powder.

2. Add the spice and apricots. Use a big spoon to mix them in very well.

3. Beat the milk, butter, egg, lemon juice and sugar in another bowl.

4. Use a spoon to make a large hole in the middle of the flour mixture.

You could add glacé cherries, instead of apricots.

Heat the oven to gas mark 4, 180°C, 350°F

7. Bake for about 20-25 minutes, until the tops are golden brown.

5. Pour in half of the beaten mixture. Stir it well. Pour in the rest and mix gently.

6. Put a tablespoon of mix in each hole in the tin. Don't smooth the tops.

You can also make these muffins with chocolate chips, but miss out the spice.

8. Leave the muffins in the tin for five minutes. Put them on a rack to cool.

Flower sweets

You will need:
275g (10oz) icing sugar, sifted
half the white of a small egg, beaten
(or dried egg white,
mix as directed on the packet)
juice of ¼ lemon
1 teaspoon of peppermint flavouring
yellow and red food dyes
a tray covered in plastic foodwrap
small flower cutter

  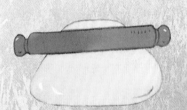

1. Sift the icing sugar into a deep bowl. Make a hole in the middle of it with a spoon.

2. In a small bowl, mix the egg white, lemon juice and the peppermint. Pour it into the sugar.

3. Use a blunt knife to stir the mixture. Then squeeze it between your fingers until it is smooth.

4. Cut the mixture into three pieces of the same size. Put each piece into a bowl.

5. Put a few drops of red food dye into one of the bowls. Use a metal spoon to mix it well.

6. Put a few drops of yellow food dye into one of the other bowls. Mix it in very well.

7. Sprinkle a little icing sugar on a work surface. Roll the yellow mixture until it is this thick.

8. Use a cutter to cut out as many flowers as you can. Cut them close together.

9. Use a blunt knife to lift the flowers onto a baking tray. Make red flowers in the same way.

10. Pull off a piece of white mixture about this size. Roll it in your hands to make a ball.

11. Press the ball to flatten it a little then press it into the middle of a flower shape.

12. Make lots more white balls and press them into the middles of the flowers.

13. Leave the flowers on the tray for at least an hour until they become hard.

Put some sweets into a box for a present.

Hot bunnies

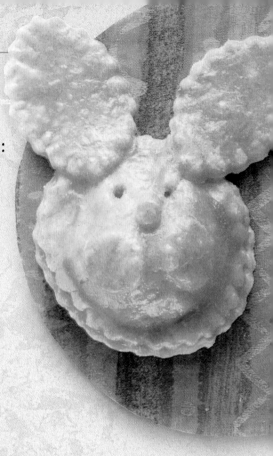

For four bunnies, you will need:
For the pastry:
150g (6oz) plain flour
75g (3oz) margarine
6 teaspoons of very
cold water
pinch of salt

For the filling:
50g (2oz) sausage meat
1 egg, beaten
large round cutter
bottle top
fat straw
greased baking tray

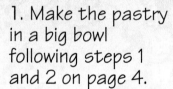

1. Make the pastry in a big bowl following steps 1 and 2 on page 4.

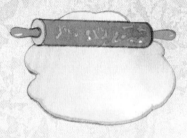

2. Sprinkle some flour onto a work surface. Roll out the pastry thinly.

3. Cut three circles with the cutter and two with the bottle top, for each rabbit.

4. Roll four very small balls of pastry. These will be noses.

5. Use a pastry brush to paint one of the large circles with beaten egg.

6. Put a big teaspoon of sausage meat in the middle.

7. Lay one of the big circles on top and flatten it gently with your hand.

8. Press your finger all around the edge to join the circles.

   Heat the oven to gas mark 6, 200°C, 400°F

9. Brush the tops with egg. Lift them onto the baking tray with a fish slice.

10. Press on two of the small bottle-top circles for cheeks. Add a nose.

11. Cut one ear by pressing the cutter half way across one of the big circles.

12. Cut another ear from the other side of the of the circle.

13. Press the ears at the top. Brush the ears, nose and cheeks with egg.

14. Make two eyes by pushing the end of the straw into the pastry.

To make a pig, cut out the ears and nose with the bottle top. Cut nostrils with a straw.

15. Bake in the oven for about 15 minutes or until they are golden.

19

Crown cake

For the cake, you will need:
100g (4oz) soft margarine
100g (4oz) caster sugar
100g (4oz) self-raising flour
2 eggs
20cm (8in) cake tin

For the decoration:
8 cone wafers
ribbon
glacé cherries
bright sweets

For the butter icing:
75g (3oz) soft butter
150g (6oz) icing sugar
lemon juice

To make the cake

1. Mix the sugar and margarine well until the mixture goes creamy.

2. Beat one of the eggs and a little flour into the mixture.

3. Add the other egg and some more flour. Beat them in.

4. Gently mix in the rest of the flour with a metal spoon.

5. Grease the tin. Spoon the mixture in. Bake for about 40-45 minutes.

6. Leave for three to four minutes, then turn the cake out onto a cooling rack.

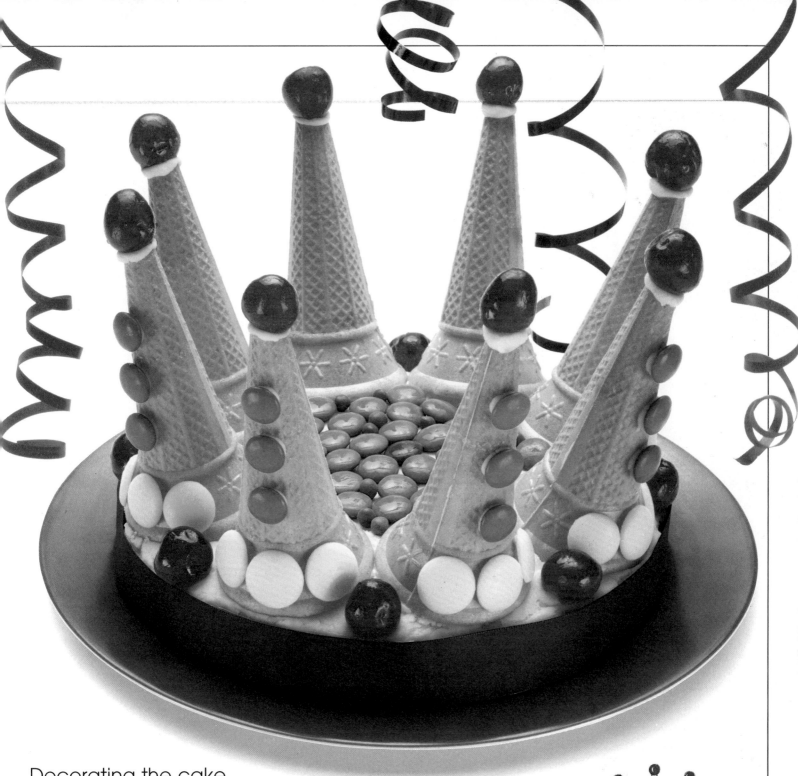

Decorating the cake

7. Make the icing by mixing the butter and icing sugar. Add a few drops of lemon juice.

8. Put a tablespoon of icing in a bowl. Spread the rest on top. Decorate the middle with sweets.

9. Pinch the ends off the cones. Press them on. Wrap some ribbon around the cake and tape it.

10. Dip the cherries in the spare icing. Press one on each cone. Add more cherries and sweets.

Little cheese tarts

For about 12 tarts, you will need:
150g (6oz) plain flour
75g (3oz) margarine
6 teaspoons of very cold water
pinch of salt
small tin of sweetcorn, drained
50g (2oz) cheese, grated
1 egg
3 tablespoons of milk
round cutter
greased baking tray with shallow pans

1. Make some pastry in a big bowl following steps 1 and 2 on page 4.

2. Sprinkle a little flour onto a work surface. Roll out the pastry thinly.

3. Cut out 12 circles with the cutter. Cut them close together.

4. Grease the baking tray. Press the circles gently into the tray.

5. Put a heaped teaspoon of sweetcorn into each one.

6. Sprinkle some grated cheese on top of the sweetcorn.

7. Beat the egg and the milk in a jug. Pour a little into each tart.

8. Bake them for 15-20 minutes until they are golden and puffy.

9. Lift the tarts onto a rack and leave them for a little while to cool.

You can eat the tarts when they are either warm or cold.

Heat the oven to gas mark 5, 190°C, 375 °F

Painted biscuits

To make about 20 biscuits you will need:
50g (2oz) icing sugar, sifted
75g (3oz) soft margarine
the yolk from a large egg
vanilla essence
150g (6oz) plain flour, sifted
cutters
greased baking tray

To decorate the biscuits:
beaten egg yolk
food dyes

1. Mix the icing sugar and the margarine until they are smooth.

2. Mix in the egg yolk, stirring it well. Add a few drops of vanilla essence.

3. Hold a sieve over the bowl and pour in the flour. Shake it through the sieve.

4. Mix the flour in with a wooden spoon until you get a smooth dough.

5. Wrap the dough in foodwrap. Put it in a freezer while you mix the dyes.

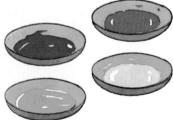

6. Put some egg yolk onto saucers. Mix a few drops of food dye with each.

7. Roll out half the dough quite thinly on a floury surface. Then roll the rest.

8. Use big cutters to press out shapes. Cut them close together.

9. Use a fish slice to lift the biscuits carefully onto a baking tray.

10. Press lightly with small cutters to make patterns on the biscuits.

11. Use a very clean paintbrush to paint shapes with the dyes.

12. Bake them for 10-12 minutes. Let them cool a little. Put them on a rack.

Decorate your biscuits with lots of different patterns.

This makes lots of biscuits so you could freeze some of the dough to use another day.

Coconut mice

For eight large mice, three medium mice, three
baby mice and eight pieces of cheese, you will need:
250g (10oz) icing sugar
200g (8oz) tin of condensed milk
175g (7oz) desiccated coconut
red and yellow food dyes
red liquorice 'bootlaces' or thick yarn
silver cake decorating balls
sweets for ears

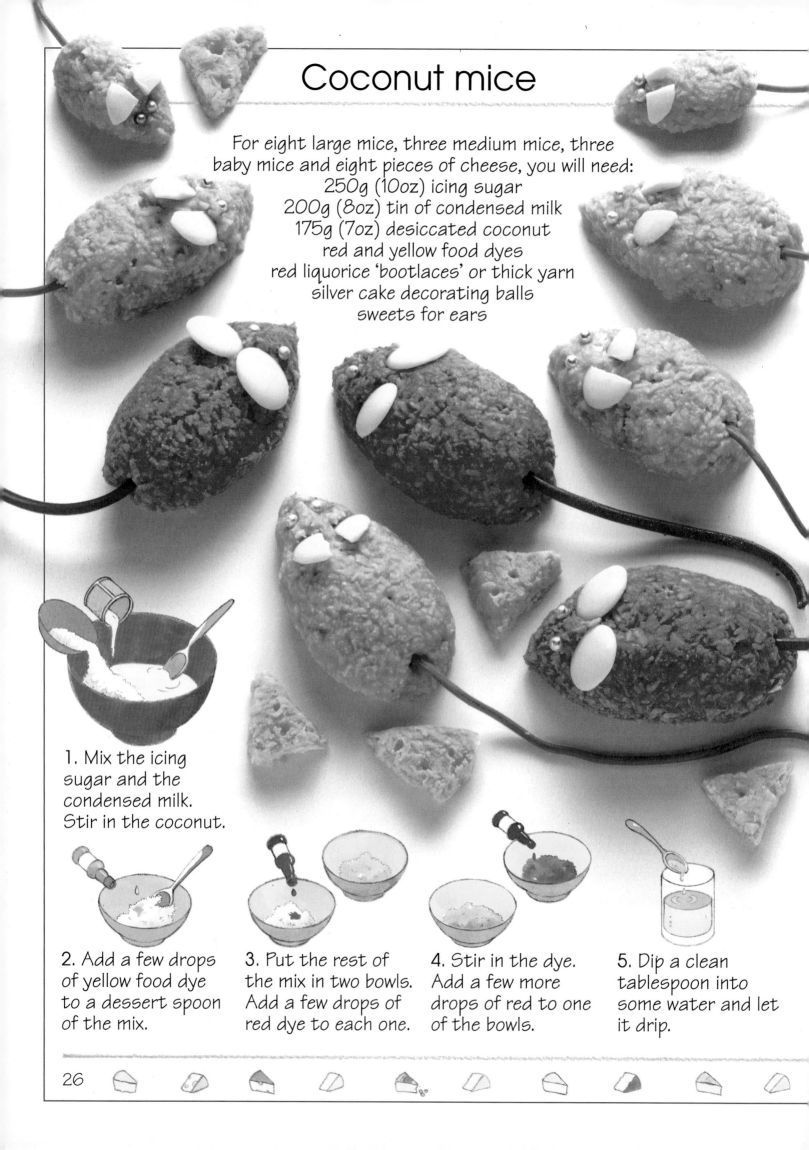

1. Mix the icing
sugar and the
condensed milk.
Stir in the coconut.

2. Add a few drops
of yellow food dye
to a dessert spoon
of the mix.

3. Put the rest of
the mix in two bowls.
Add a few drops of
red dye to each one.

4. Stir in the dye.
Add a few more
drops of red to one
of the bowls.

5. Dip a clean
tablespoon into
some water and let
it drip.

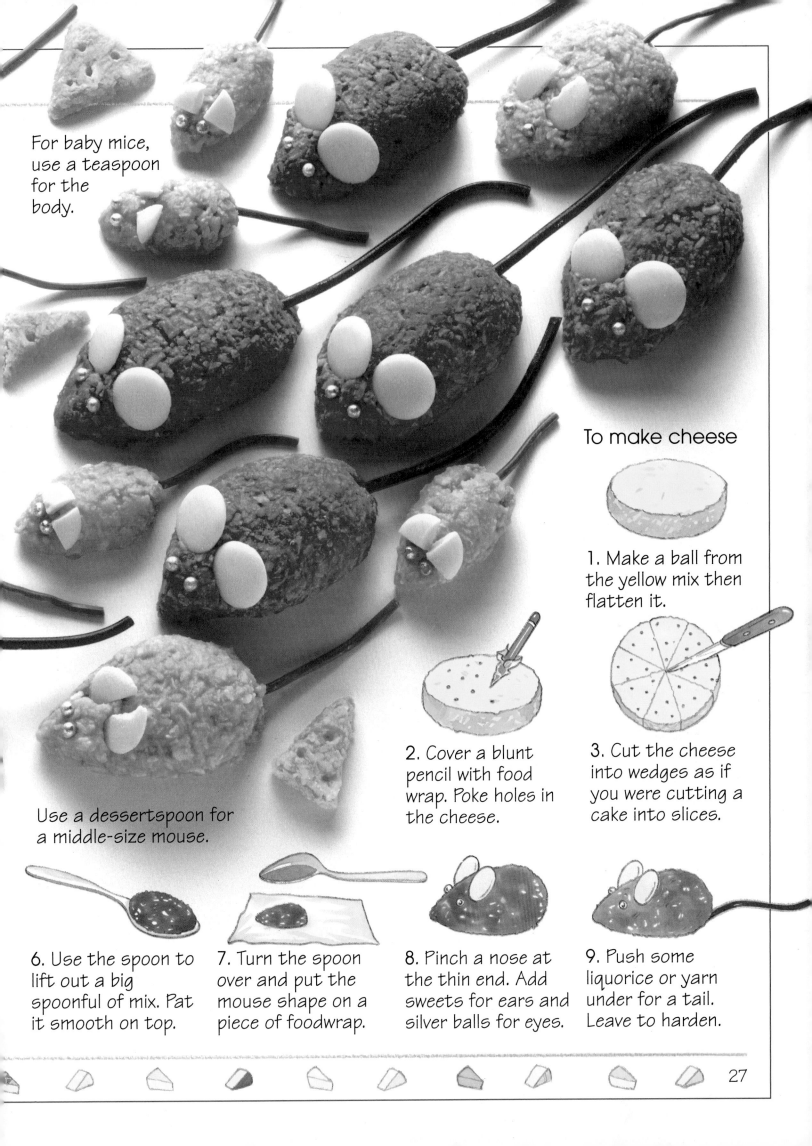

For baby mice, use a teaspoon for the body.

Use a dessertspoon for a middle-size mouse.

To make cheese

1. Make a ball from the yellow mix then flatten it.

2. Cover a blunt pencil with food wrap. Poke holes in the cheese.

3. Cut the cheese into wedges as if you were cutting a cake into slices.

6. Use the spoon to lift out a big spoonful of mix. Pat it smooth on top.

7. Turn the spoon over and put the mouse shape on a piece of foodwrap.

8. Pinch a nose at the thin end. Add sweets for ears and silver balls for eyes.

9. Push some liquorice or yarn under for a tail. Leave to harden.

Easy pizza

Cheese and sweetcorn

For one 25cm (10in) pizza you will need:
225g (8oz) plain flour
½ teaspoon of salt
2 tablespoons of oil
150ml (¼pt) of milk
75g (3oz) cheese, grated
4 tomatoes, thinly sliced
a pinch of mixed dried herbs

Topping ideas:
sliced mushrooms
sweetcorn
(tinned or frozen)
pineapple
chopped ham
pepperoni

1. Sift the flour and salt together in a big bowl. Make a hole in the middle with a spoon.

2. Mix the milk with the oil in a jug. Mix it well. Pour it carefully into the hole in the flour.

Pepperoni, mushroom and cheese

Heat the oven to gas mark 6, 200°C, 400°F

3. Use a blunt knife to stir the mixture well, until it makes a sticky dough.

4. Sprinkle a little flour onto a work surface. Roll the dough into a circle as wide as this page.

6. Add more toppings if you want. Bake on the top shelf for 15-20 minutes.

5. Cover the dough with the sliced tomatoes. Sprinkle the cheese on top. Add the herbs.

Chopped ham, cheese and tomato

Sweetcorn, cheese and pineapple

Christmas tree cakes

For about 15 cakes, you will need:
100g (4oz) self-raising flour
100g (4oz) soft margarine
100g (4oz) sugar
2 eggs
paper cake cases
baking tray with shallow pans
assorted sweets

For the butter icing:
50g (2oz) butter or margarine, softened
100g (4oz) icing sugar, sifted
food dye
squeeze of lemon juice or a few drops of
vanilla essence

1. Follow steps 1 and 2 on page 10 to make a sponge mixture.

2. Put the cases in a baking tray. Half-fill each one with sponge mixture.

3. Bake them for about 20 minutes. Leave them on a rack to cool.

4. To make the butter icing, stir the butter until it is creamy.

5. Add some of the icing sugar. Stir it in. Mix in the rest, a little at a time.

6. Stir in a few drops of food dye and the lemon juice or vanilla.

7. Spread some icing on top of each cake. Put a sweet in the middle.

8. Put small sweets around the middle one to make a pattern.

  Heat the oven to gas mark 5, 190°C, 375°F

Use bright sweets to make different patterns on your cakes.

Sunshine toast

You will need:
1 slice of bread
margarine
1 medium or small egg
large cutter
baking tray

1. Dip a piece of kitchen paper into some margarine and rub it all over a baking tray.

2. Spread margarine on one side of the bread. Press the cutter hard in the middle of the bread.

3. Lift out the shape you have cut. Lay the pieces of bread on the tray, with the butter up.

4. Break the egg onto a saucer. Carefully slide the egg into the hole you have cut.

5. Bake for seven minutes on the top shelf of an oven, or for a little longer if you don't like a runny yolk.

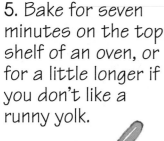

6. Lift the pieces of bread carefully off the tray. Eat it while it is warm.

Heat the oven to gas mark 6, 200°C, 400°F

This edition first published in 2002 by Usborne Publishing Ltd., Usborne House, 83-85 Saffron Hill, London EC1N 8RT, England. www.usborne.com Copyright © 2002, 1996 Usborne Publishing Ltd. The name Usborne and the devices ♀☿ are Trade Marks of Usborne Publishing Ltd. All rights reserved.